My Grandpa's Monster Toes

Ikea Chapman
Asante Sharp

My Grandpa Has Monster Toes

Copyright © 2021 Ikea Chapman and Asante Sharp.

All rights reserved. No part of this book may be used or reproduced by any means, graphic, electronic, or mechanical, including photocopying, recording, taping or by any information storage retrieval system without the written permission of the author except in the case of brief quotations embodied in critical articles and reviews.

iUniverse books may be ordered through booksellers or by contacting:

iUniverse
1663 Liberty Drive
Bloomington, IN 47403
www.iuniverse.com
844-349-9409

Because of the dynamic nature of the Internet, any web addresses or links contained in this book may have changed since publication and may no longer be valid. The views expressed in this work are solely those of the author and do not necessarily reflect the views of the publisher, and the publisher hereby disclaims any responsibility for them.

Any people depicted in stock imagery provided by Getty Images are models, and such images are being used for illustrative purposes only.
Certain stock imagery © Getty Images.

ISBN: 978-1-6632-1631-1 (sc)
978-1-6632-1632-8 (e)

Library of Congress Control Number: 2021901274

Print information available on the last page.

iUniverse rev. date: 01/30/2021

Dedication

Robert E. Reeves, for you inspire us to be above and beyond our imagination.

I want to tell you a tale about a time when I discovered my grandpa had monster toes.

I'm serious! It all started about two weeks ago. My baby sister A'Mia and I spent the night at my grandparent's house.

My mommy had to work. At least that what she said but maybe it was to get some mommy time. Anyway, I enjoyed visiting my grandparent's they're the coolest. I swear!

Are you ready? This is some creepy stuff! I am just trying to warn you.

"Asante!" My mommy called out wanting me to pack my bag. So, she can help my little sister get ready. We were planning to spend the weekend with my grandparents.

"Okay," I said because I was so excited. I was ready to eat whatever Be Be cooked. That is my grandma. I knew she was going to have my favorite food, shrimp, chicken wings, and pizza with olives. So yummy!

As we were headed that way, I had the urge to bring my favorite toy, "Blue Ninja". He's the best superhero on the planet! He has super speed. I am going to be like him when I get older. You'll see!

We arrived at my grandparent's house.

"Hey Tae and Mia!" That's what Be Be called us.

"Hey Be Be," I said and darted straight into my grandpa room. I kept all my junk food and toys in grandpa's room. That our secret, do not tell my Be Be or Mommy.

As I entered my grandpa's room, I noticed it was darker than usual. So, I tried turning on the night light, but it did not work. Oh gosh! I hate the dark. It reminds me of creepy and scary things. So, I knew I had to get Blue Ninja, he will help me defeat my fears.

I re-enter the room, grandpa was laying on his large bed in silence. "Hey, grandpa, are you sleeping?" I asked with caution.

No answer.

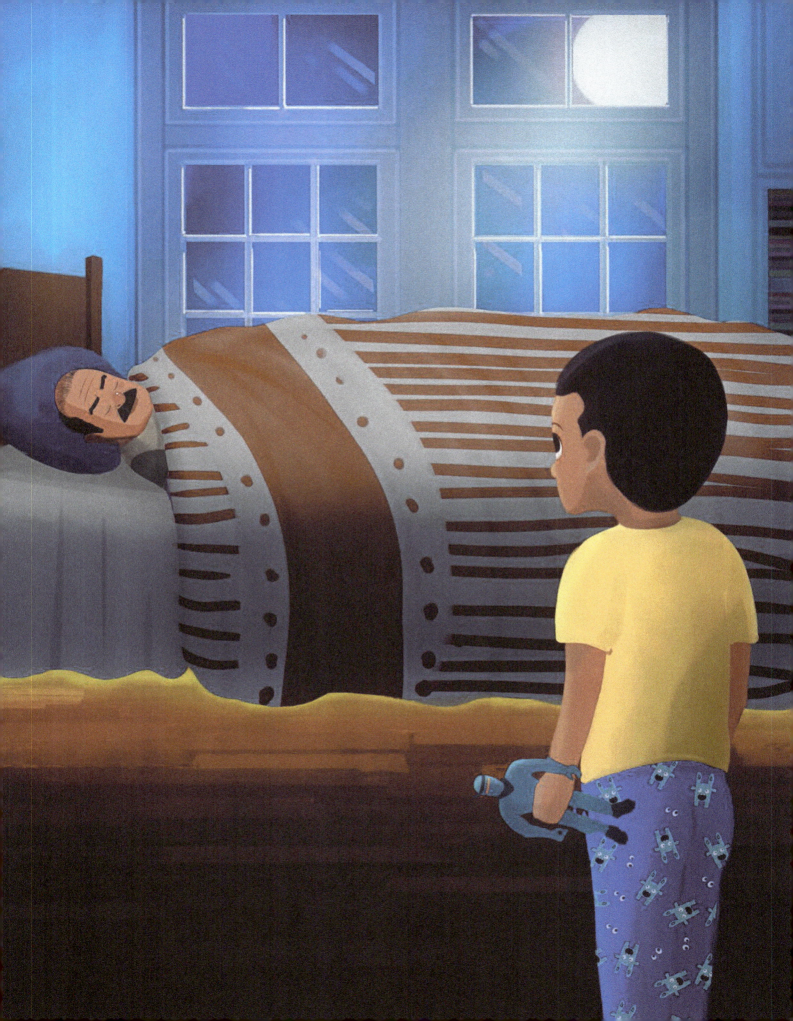

So, I began to jump into grandpa's bed. "Ouch!" Grandpa hollered as I landed directly on his toes.

oooucchh

At that moment, I had no idea about the transformation that was about to start. I knew Blue Ninja and I were about to fight something very strange and paranormal.

I held Blue Ninja very tight and glanced at the most horrific sight in my life. Grandpa's monster toe's!

His toes were the ugliest thing I had ever seen. Straight out of a horror movie. "Oh gosh!"

His toes barked a gruesome sound that I'd never even heard before. Grandpa's feet were lumpy, black, green, and blue as if they had been frost bitten and zombie turned. One or two toes was missing from each side.

"Pow!" Blue Ninja and I began throwing punches as if we were Mike Tyson trying to win a boxing championship. His toes were trying to shoot out alien slime on me and Blue Ninja.

"Agrh!" His toes moaned as the punches were becoming more severe. I was not letting those toes eat me. No way!

"Asante! Asante! Aasssaannttttteeeee!" Be Be hollered.

I was afraid to answer the calls Be Be made out to me. But I realized I had to come up with a plan to finish off those toes. Before Be Be called me again. I could not let them defeat me or Blue Ninja, but most of all my grandpa.

Eventually, his toes were defeated. But my grandpa still did not wake up.

"Asante!" I heard coming through the bedroom door.

I knew it was Be Be's voice. But I did not care if I was in trouble. The monster toes had destroyed my grandpa. I was sad and disappointed and could tell Blue Ninja was too.

Asante!!

I wiped my tears and ran towards the bedroom door, Be Be could save grandpa, she is old and smart.

"Yes!" I'm coming!" I hollered and ran. I was so eager to get help.

"Huh!" I said in confusion. I was in grandpa's room laying in his large bed with Blue Ninja and my cool monster pajamas. But the weirdest thing happened. My grandpa was not around.

Moments later.
Be Be was holding Mia with grandpa by her side. They towered me and Blue Ninja, with a look of concern.

"Are you okay?" They both asked, at that moment I realized it was all a dream, Grandpa's monster toes!

I told grandpa that I loved him, and we ate my shrimp, chicken wings, and pizza with olives.

So, the moral of this story is do not have crazy nightmares of your grandpa toes. Or they might come after you.

CPSIA information can be obtained
at www.ICGtesting.com
Printed in the USA
LVHW071151090221
678815LV00021B/621